THE WAY HOME
&
THE BITTERSWEET SUMMER

ANDY RUNTON

OWLY:

THE WAY HOME & THE BITTERSWEET SUMMER

ISBN 1-891830-62-7

1. ALL-AGES
2. ORNITHOLOGY
3. GRAPHIC NOVELS

TOP SHELF PRODUCTIONS
P.O. BOX 1282
MARIETTA, GA 30061-1282
U.S.A.

WWW.TOPSHELFCOMIX.COM

PUBLISHED BY TOP SHELF PRODUCTIONS, INC.
PUBLISHERS: CHRIS STAROS AND BRETT WARNOCK.

EDITED BY CHRIS STAROS & ROBERT VENDITTI

SECOND PRINTING, JANUARY 2006
PRINTED IN CANADA

OTHER BOOKS BY ANDY RUNTON:

OWLY: VOLUME TWO, JUST A LITTLE BLUE
ISBN 1-891830-64-3

OWLY: VOLUME THREE, FLYING LESSONS
ISBN 1-891830-76-7

FOR MY MOM

WHO BROUGHT THE JOY
OF THE LITTLE BIRDS
INTO MY LIFE.

CONTENTS

SPECIAL THANKS TO
CHRIS, BRETT, AND ROB,
AND TO MY FAMILY,
FRIENDS, FELLOW ARTISTS,
AND ALL OF THE OWLY FANS
FOR THEIR ENCOURAGEMENT,
KINDNESS, AND SUPPORT.

THE WAY HOME

RUSTLE
RUSTLE

!
seed

seed

DINK
DINK

DINK
DINK

DINK
DINK

?

SEED

DRIP

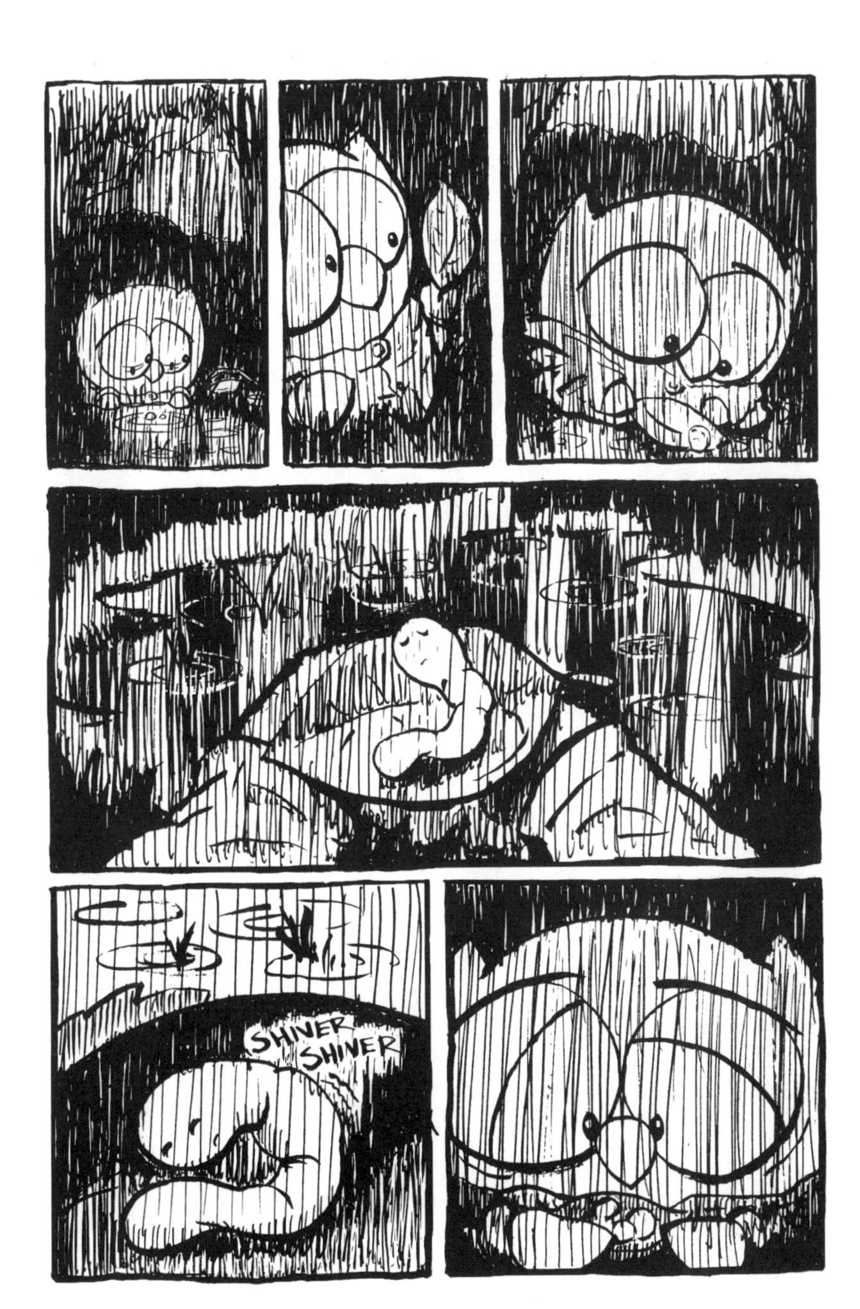
SHIVER
SHIVER

SHIVER
SHIVER

zzz

OWLY

DRIP

SPLASH!
!
!
!

WORMIES

?

MAP

MAP

SOAP
MAP

MAP

SHAKE
SHAKE

?

WO RMIES

DUST
DUST
SNIFF
SNIFF
SNIFF
SNIFF

KNOCK
KNOCK
KNOCK

SLAM!

!

. . .
SHAKE
SHAKE

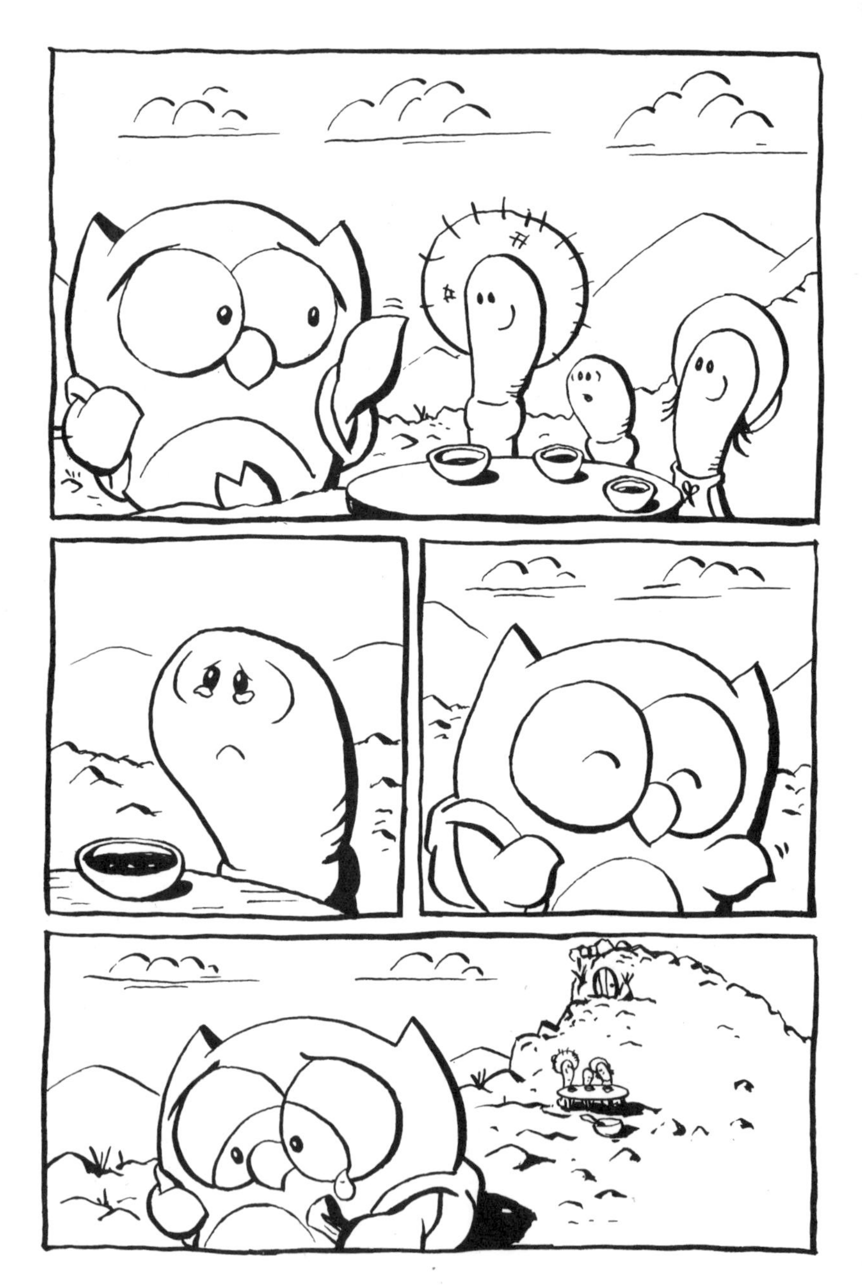

SCRUNCH
SCRUNCH
SCRUNCH
SCRUNCH
SCRUNCH
SCRUNCH

THE
END

THE BITTERSWEET SUMMER

HMMM

HMM

HMMMMM

MMMZZZ
!!!

HMMMMMM

MMMZZZT

LITTLE SEEDS
FOR LITTLE BIRDIES

HMMMMMMM

HMMMMMM

HMMMMMM

HMMMMMM

HMMMM

SMALL BIRDS

!

HUMMINGBIRDS
THE SMALLEST OF ALL BIRDS IS THE HUMMINGBIRD. THESE TINY JEWELS, WITH THEIR
A MALE RUBY-THROAT HUMMINGBIRD IN FLIGHT.
FEMALE RUBY-THROAT AT A TRUMPET VINE BLOSSOM.
HUMMINGBIRDS DO NOT FEED ON SEEDS AND BERRIES LIKE OTHER SMALL BIRDS. INSTEAD, THEY FEED ON NECTAR FROM FLOWERS.
!

CLINKA

CLINKA
CLINKA
CLINKA

NURSERY

$$
$$

LOCAL FLOWERS
$$

NECTAR FLOWERS

LANTANA
BLOOMS ALL SUMMER!
FULL SUN/PARTIAL SHADE
$1.00

SALVIA
HUMMINGBIRD FAVORITE!

HMMMMMMM

HMMMMM

SQUEAK
SQUEAK

HMMMM

HMM

MMMMM

SHAKE
SHAKE

OWLY

HMMMMM

??!?
GULP

RUSTLE
RUSTLE

!

SLIP

RUSTLE RUSTLE

RUSTLE
RUSTLE

?

CLICK!

CRASH!

TRIP!

THUD!

?!

!

CREAK

CLICK!

Owly's
friends
owly

Tiny, Wormy, and Angel
June 3rd

Tiny, Angel, and Me
June 3rd

Angel and Tiny both have their favorite flowers. ☺
Tiny prefers a new flower (a butterfly bush) while Angel still prefers the Salvia.
July 10th

Angel likes to sit under the water while I give the plants a drink.
August 23rd

Tiny conserves his energy by sitting down for dinner at the Lantana.

Angel and wormy play hide and seek in the flowers.

September 23rd

Wormy and me in our
hummingbird garden.

Seeing our little friends
always makes me happy.

October 5th

OCTOBER

TAP
TAP

SHIVER
SHIVER

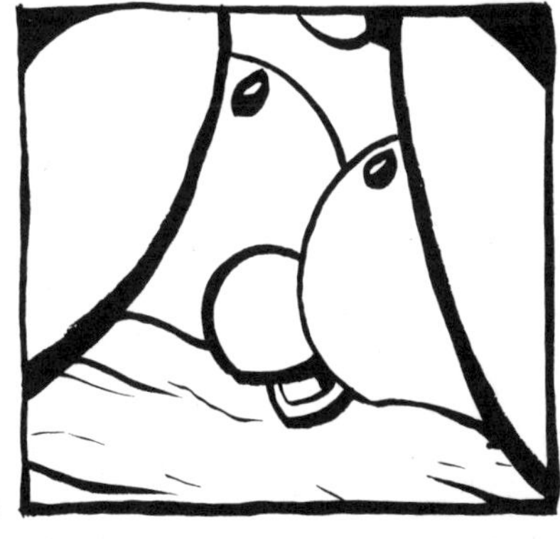

SHIVER
SHIVER

?

TIE TIE TIE

!

!

THUMP
THUMP

HMMRPH
MMRPH

FLUFF
FLUFF
FLUFF
FLUFF

!

??
??

NURSERY
?

NURSERY

LOCAL
FLOWERS

NECTAR
FLOWERS

?

APRIL
...

NOVEMBER

HMMMMMM

?!
?!

?
FLOWER SEEDS

FLOWER SEEDS

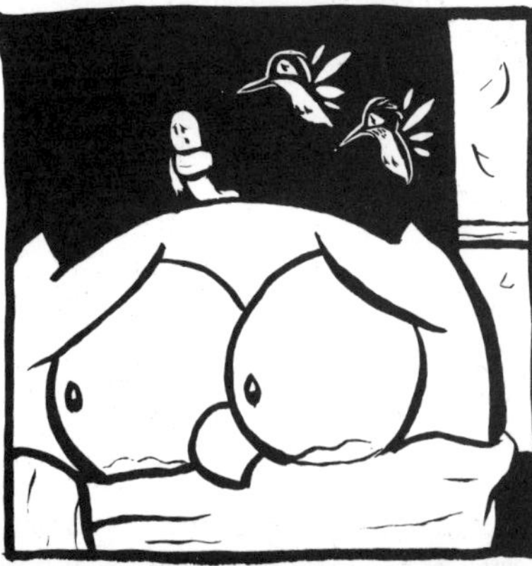

SQUEAK
SQUEAK

SNIFFLE
SNIFFLE

!

OWLY

HUMMINGBIRDS

HUMMINGBIRDS
AS WINTER APPROACHES, THE HUMMINGBIRDS MIGRATE SOUTH FOLLOWING THE BLOOMING FLOWERS.
THEY SPEND THE COLD WINTER MONTHS IN SUNNY SOUTH AMERICA. MANY OF THE HUMMINGBIRDS EVEN FLY NON-STOP ACROSS THE GULF OF MEXICO TO REACH THEIR WARM WINTER HOME.
MANY
HUMMIN
FEED
INCL
" NE
TTLE
US
RUBY

EVEN THOUGH THESE LITTLE BIRDS MUST LEAVE US IN WINTERTIME, AS SOON AS THE FLOWERS BEGIN TO BLOOM IN THE SPRING THE HUMMINGBIRDS WILL RETURN. THEY HAVE AN EXCELLENT MEMORY AND ALWAYS RETURN TO THE SAME SPRINGTIME HOME.
MALE RUBY THROAT
FEMALE RUBY THROAT ON HER NEST

NOVEMBER
SEEDS

DECEMBER

JANUARY

FEBRUARY

MARCH

APRIL

WELCOME!

THE END

 : ANDYRUNTON@MAC.COM

 : ANDY RUNTON
5502 EAST WIND DR.
LILBURN, GA 30047-6410
U.S.A.

WWW.ANDYRUNTON.COM